FREEDOM TRAIL

BRENDA G. UNSWORTH

Inquiries and Book Orders should be addressed to:

Great Writers Media
Email: info@greatwritersmedia.com
Phone: 877-600-5469

ISBN: 978-1-960939-00-5 (sc)
ISBN: 978-1-960939-01-2 (ebk)

CONTENTS

In memory of my late husband, Peter Unsworth, who taught me that anything is possible.

Dedicated to my son Paul, who believes in me as much as I believe in him.

<h1>CHAPTER 1</h1>

THE PRESIDENT OF THE NEW REPUBLIC WAS ASSASSINATED TODAY at 15.00 hours world time. He was found lying in a pool of blood outside the remains of the palace.

There had been no noise, no disturbance, and no shouts of frustration, just total silence. People were passing by looking down at the young body, paying no attention to who was lying in total darkness.

"Have you heard the news? The president's dead. We rule the country now. No hypocrite of a president for us, the New Polity of Today," said Slyster with a satisfied grin. "Freedom. Total freedom."

Government bodies were to be formed, and many were needed.

Communication was now a big problem. Electricity supplies were low, and the only means of keeping in touch was to travel on foot.

Edification was a thing of the past. The education system was long gone.

The youth had rebelled, and now anarchy, strife, greed, and selfishness were the main modes of human survival. Now that the president was dead, nothing could stop them.

Curane and Slyster started towards the tower where Tyler had been living for the past two years. It was ideal for water and prospects. As they entered the tower, they shouted up the spiral staircase. It was made of Perspex, so Tyler was able to learn of any unwanted visitors.

There was silence. "Tyler, are you there?" Tyler was nowhere to be seen. Slyster began to climb the staircase when Curane grabbed his arm. He fell backwards with a balance he was unable to control. Curane screamed for him to run.

She began to flee the tower, but Slyster was unable to follow her. He felt a sudden pain in his leg and fell to the ground, from where he found himself staring upwards into the eyes of a support officer, the latter's weapon pointing into his face. The officer's yellow uniform was of a distinguishing source.

"We are going to rule this country now, not you. We have been waiting for this moment for years. Don't even think about trying to get up, because I am going to incinerate you as soon as you move."

Slyster lay frozen with eyes wide and mouth agape. He tried not to breathe. His heart was pounding, and he thought the support officer might be able to hear it.

"Don't move, I said." "I'm not."

A loud noise was heard from above, and the support officer raised his head upwards. Slyster kicked the weapon he was holding from his hand across to the other end of the stairway just as Tyler came hurtling down the staircase. He ran into the officer at great speed and swept him across the staircase.

The officer landed on his back with his arms waving in the air. "I will get you for this." He tried to stand upright, his body sliding across the Perspex.

Slyster went for the weapon. He pointed it at the officer and looked at his drawn, worn-out expression. Slyster pushed the muzzle, and the yellow uniform turned into a pile of ashes.

"Curane! She's bolted."

Slyster and Tyler ran towards the entrance of the tower. Curane was outside, curled up into a ball, her head shaking with fear. She began to sob loudly.

Slyster held his hand out towards her. As he pulled her towards him to hold her tight, she began to retaliate. She pushed Slyster away from her and raised herself from the floor, pressing her hands to her head.

Tyler was trying to approach her to comfort her in some way.

"No, Tyler, I cannot do this any more. Besides, who is going to help us now? Everyone is glad the president is dead, but who really cares what happens now?"

Curane lifted herself up and walked away as the two men decided to head back into the tower.

Slyster looked behind and could see Curane vanishing into the distance, towards what they now regarded to be their place.

"Tyler, it's Curane. She seems to have lost a lot of enthusiasm. She used to be so lively, so full of life. Nothing seemed to get her down. Now everything seems to get to her."

Tyler looked at Slyster and frowned. "No, not Curane. She's a survivor— self-reliant and stubborn about it. She'll be fine."

Tyler walked towards the bathroom. From the open cabinet, he pulled out a monitor. It was scratched and dented, but he had plans for this piece of old machinery.

"If I can find some loose wire, I may be able to connect this up to the monitors outside and link it to the intercom system."

He proceeded to disassemble the monitor and retrieve some ends of electrical wiring.

"Oh, I'll leave you to it, Tyler. I'll go and see where Curane's hidden herself."

"I'll catch you later."

Slyster left the tower block. He ran towards the building that he and Curane were using for sleeping quarters. As he approached, he could see Curane walking in the distance. He ran after her.

"Curane, don't give up now. Tyler's going to fix up his old monitor and see if he can contact some of our old friends. Come on, we'll have more help now."

"I'm sorry, Sly. I was being stupid."

Slyster held his hand out to her, and she took it. They clasped their fingers around each other's and walked towards their home.

"When two become one," he said.

"When two become one" was her reply. It was something they said to each other after an argument. It made them feel better.

"I just need some sleep. I'm so tired; I just can't think any more."

On entering the room, Curane lay herself down onto a large piece of wooden frame covered with feathers sewn into some old sacking they had found.

"Try and get some sleep," Sly said in a quiet whisper as he stroked her hair and moved it away from her eyes. He kissed her forehead, and she closed her eyes. "Don't worry any more. Everything is going to be OK now."

He knew that everything wasn't going to be OK, but he wanted Curane to calm down. He pulled up a bench and sat at the window. He could see Tyler's tower in the distance lit up like a lighthouse. He thought Tyler should really try to save some power.

People were walking around in a disturbed manner and chanting strange noises. Fires were smouldering in the distance; people were burning whatever they could just to keep warm. It was a cold night, and the air smelt of smoke from weeks gone by.

Sly turned to look at Curane. She was sleeping soundly. Maybe she was right. Perhaps there was no point in going on.

If the support officers wanted to rule the country, why not let them? Perhaps they couldn't do any more damage than what had already been done. Sly dismissed these thoughts from his mind as quickly as they had come. He knew that the law was now corrupt and only the New Polity of Today could save them.

He slept on the bench, curled up into a small shape, not wanting to disturb Curane. He awoke to a stiff neck. His back was feeling the pain of weeks gone by. *I must sort myself out,* he thought to himself.

"It's me, Sly. Let me in—quick."

It was Tyler. He had called with the monitor, which was being carried by a second person Sly had not met before.

"This is Idle. He reckons he can help us. Without venturing outside, we should all be able to keep in touch."

Idle began to strip wires, and the monitor was soon in place. He seemed to be interested in getting things done quickly and correctly. He smiled at Curane, who had suddenly awakened and had just begun to feel herself again. It was good to have another person around, someone who could help and who seemed to know what they were doing.

"Right, that's done. I'll go over to the tower now and see if this thing can be connected up. We should be able to see each other, but the transmission will be very poor."

Idle left the building. "You OK now, Curane?" Tyler smiled with uncertainty, and she smiled back.

They watched the monitor to see if there was any sign of life. Nothing was happening. The power source was lower than ever, and all was not well.

CHAPTER 2

"CURANE, I HAVE TO LEAVE FOR A FEW DAYS. I WANT YOU TO stay here with Tyler and Idle. I need to go and see some groups from the other side of the island. They live inside Crombie Mountain. The more we have to keep us together, the stronger we will be against the support officers. They seem to be increasing in numbers. Everywhere you look, you see these yellow shapes of all different sizes. Will you do that, Curane? Will you stay here?"

"No. No, I will not stay here with those two idiots."

"Curane, that's enough. They are not idiots. It wasn't their fault the power failed."

Tyler was right; she was stubborn. "You unyielding obstinate person." "I'm not."

"Look, Curane, I don't want you to walk all that way. You haven't even got any decent footwear."

"I have somewhere."

Curane proceeded to hunt around, throwing bits of objects everywhere. She retrieved some shoes and squeezed her large feet into them. They must have been at least two sizes too small.

"There! See, I knew I had some." Her face was smiling with glee, yet one could sense that her toes were not altogether happy.

Slyster knew he was fighting a losing battle. He began to question his logic. He wondered why he hadn't just said, *Come on, Curane, let's go.* Her clothes were on, and she proceeded to open the door.

"What about food, drink, and other necessities of life?" Slyster asked.

"Oh, we can pick them up on the way. Don't you know? It's a free-for-all now.

"Yes, I know that, Curane, but we might as well take what little we have here."

Slyster began to fill his carrier. He tied it around his waist, and then he and Curane set off hand in hand.

It was raining; the weather was damp and cold. People were gathering around fires to keep warm. Old, empty, burnt tins of solid nourishment were cluttered around areas of ash. Buildings, monuments, and homes were smouldering in the distance.

"Sly, remember when we used to walk in the forests and climb when we were children? Listen to the quietness of the air. No birds to be heard. No children to be seen running around. Everything is just so morbid."

"Yeah, I miss my family, Curane." Slyster's family had been murdered in the revolution, along with millions of others.

How it began, no one really knows. The youth of today were on the rampage due to unemployment and lack of skills. Drugs and boredom set into the majority of delinquents, and looting, arson, and psychological matters had become a huge problem. The support officers had become the enforcers. They had now taken control and were dictating what happened in the country. War had broken out between the youth and the support officers, and the elderly were just past caring. People over juvenile age were too weak to survive. Many had been murdered trying to save their spouses and offspring.

Curane had no family. In fact, she never knew her parentage. Rumour had it she was cloned and sold to the highest bidder at an early age. No person had ever been important in her life. Slyster seemed to be the only person she was ever close to. They grew up together and had the same people around them most of their life, and Slyster's family were the nearest she'd ever had to normality.

"Wouldn't it be good, Sly, if we could form some kind of peace movement and all work together at getting peace and harmony back into our lives?"

"There are too many people today, Curane, who are selfish, ignorant, and greedy. They are full of hatred and wish nothing but to survive. Something needs to be done to make people change, to make them think differently.

Maybe we should just forget the whole damn thing and let nature take its course."

"Who's giving up now?"

Curane frowned at Sly. Squeezing his arm, she pulled him along, away from all the sad memories of yesterday.

The rain had stopped, and the sky was brighter than it had been that morning.

"I was wondering, Sly. Do you think that there could be a place somewhere not affected? I mean, do you think that someone somewhere could be actually living a normal life?"

"I doubt it. This revolting fever is happening worldwide." He stared at Curane. It was a look she did not recognise. He looked disturbed about something.

In the distance a group of youths were dancing around a fire. They were singing and cheering. A yellow garment was thrown into the flames.

"We rule the country now, not the Yellow Dogs."

The flames began to rise higher. Groups were chanting, "The New Polity of Today. We rule the country now."

As they were chanting, more garments were being cast onto the fire. Shouts of hysteria were heard, louder and louder.

Curane held Sly by the arm tightly. She seemed frightened, though they had seen this many times recently.

"Yellow Dogs, Yellow Dogs. Burn, you hogs."

Sly strolled over to the group, who were now ecstatic with delight. Curane was still holding on tight. He knew the youths were affected by a substance of some sort. A young male dressed in torn black clothing offered Curane a vessel containing green liquid which she did not recognise. Her head shook in disagreement. He passed it to Sly, who decided he might smell it. "Ugh …"

Sly passed it back, his face white from the rotten odour he had inhaled through his nostrils. He wanted to vomit, but nothing was inside to escape. He began to cough with extreme pain. Curane began to worry. She held onto Sly, keeping him upright as he began to fall to the ground.

The young male in black ran towards him. He held his arm as Sly slowly fell into a heap. Sly began to cry out with pain, and tears filled his eyes.

"Stand back. I'll see to him." The young male pushed Curane to one side and bent down towards Sly. "What's he taken?"

"Nothing. "Nothing at all," came her reply.

The young male shrugged his shoulders in disbelief.

"Look, I'm telling you, whoever you are, that he's taken nothing. Now can someone tell me what was in that vessel?"

"It wasn't harmful. I think you may have a sick male on your hands." He shouted to the others to help carry Sly indoors to someplace comfortable. Sly was crying out loud. Curane could see he was suffering. She knelt down beside him and held his hand tightly.

"Here, give him this." The young man passed her a goblet containing some sort of mixture.

"What is it?" She was curious to know.

"I studied medicine at one time. Degree in medical science. Don't worry, it's safe. Make him take a small sip."

Curane gently lifted Sly's head and put the goblet to his lips. He took a small sip and swallowed eagerly. Within a few seconds, he seemed more comfortable.

"It was just an analgesic, you know, painkiller."

Curane looked into Slyster's eyes. "Are you all right, Sly?"

"Hmm … I think so. I don't know what happened. I just had this terrible pain in my gut." The expression on his face changed, and the redness of his skin appeared to normalise.

"Thanks." She smiled at the stranger, who held out his hand in friendship.

They shook hands and exchanged names.

"Toska." She repeated his name. "Tos for short."

"I never thought that Toska could be made shorter!" he shouted as he began to retrieve bottles from a broken drawer. The drawer came to pieces in his hand, and most of the bottles crashed to the floor. "Damn."

He began to pick up the pieces of broken glass from the floor. "No medicines now except a couple of bottles of tabs. I'll have to go out later and see if the drug warehouse has any left.

"You two planning on staying tonight?"

Curane looked at Slyster, who now wasn't sure what to do. He felt tired and weary. He smiled at Curane, and she nodded to Toska, indicating that they would be staying.

"Good. We can all have a drink and celebrate our new-found friendship with the New Polity of Today. You do believe in them, don't you? New young blood to organise things, change things, and see things more clearly. That's what it's all about, us."

Curane wasn't sure about Toska. She thought he was a loud person. He seemed aggressive and rude yet caring in a strange way. Selfish, extraordinarily handsome, yet boyish-looking. His blond hair made him look younger than his years with his pale complexion and light blue eyes. In fact he had the same colouring as she. Sly was dark, rugged, and mature for his age.

They all wandered out into the smoky night air.

The fire was still burning bright, and the remaining yellow garments had now been destroyed. Curane was sitting by the fire, seated on the wet damp soil, thinking about the time Slyster had bought her a present from the jewellers in the nearby town. It wasn't far away. They had travelled by monorail and enjoyed the day. It didn't seem long ago. It was five years. A lot had happened in those five years.

Slyster had lost his job, his family, and his home. Everything they had ever built together was gone now. Maybe most people had been through the same. They had! So many people had died in the fires. Many were burnt alive. Innocent people who lived good lives had perished. Life was now different. Very different.

Curane remembered the present. It was a locket made of alloy. It contained a diamond, sealed in the centre. It sparkled in the light and glistened like raindrops. It opened into a scrolled picture of Slyster and her. She cherished it. As she felt the locket between her fingers, she wished those days were still here.

She remembered a line from a poem, 'Life changes with the seasons.' She had found an old book of Slyster's father's in his room. She loved it. It was full of poetry and stories of days gone by. He'd given it to her as a gift. He knew she wanted it very much. She wondered where it was now.

The crackling of the fire became louder. A young female had thrown some refuse on top, causing a loud hissing sound.

Everyone cheered with excitement. "Drink, Curane?"

Tos handed her a bottle of mead. She liked mead; it made her relax. She drank it slowly. Her head began to whirl, and her body began to relax. Suddenly night had turned into day.

She awoke to the sound of laughter. Toska and Sly were still drinking. Having stayed awake through the night, they'd travelled to the warehouse and returned with medication of different sorts. Toska threw a small box over to Curane for her to catch. She opened it and retrieved a small ring containing a sapphire stone.

"To match your eyes!" he shouted across the room. It squeezed onto her index finger, and she smiled. The room was full of bottles, syringes, and goods taken from the warehouse.

"Curane, that ring came from the same jeweller I bought your locket from," Slyster shouted over to her.

She smiled, but really looting wasn't something she agreed with. She knew that whatever was given to her wouldn't replace the cherished items she once had. She would give the ring away if it meant having her book of poems back.

"Sly, you said something about going to find some old friends of yours. I'd like to come if you both don't mind. I need to get away from here, meet new people, see new faces and such," Toska said, peering into the bottles, inspecting them one by one, and waiting for an answer.

Curane looked at Sly. Sometimes she thought he could read her mind, or maybe it was because they had spent so much time together that they had become one. She frowned with disapproval.

"I'm not sure. What do you say, Curane?"

He'd put her in a position she could not get out of without feeling on edge. After all, Toska had given her this ring and had noticed the colour of her eyes. She turned the ring on her finger nervously. "Curane?" Sly was waiting for an answer.

"Yes! Why not? The more, the merrier." She'd read that in a book somewhere.

They collected their belongings. Tos gathered the medicines, stating that he didn't go anywhere without his "babies".

The sunshine was beating down, and thankfully the weather had changed dramatically overnight. Curane decided to remove her sweater. She draped it around her shoulders to keep the rays off her arms. The warmth made her feel alive. Today was a new day—a better day, she hoped. They had planned to trek thirty miles that day, but Curane's feet were beginning to take their toll after the first ten miles. As she sat on a large boulder by a stream, she removed her footwear and immersed her feet into the cold muddy water. She felt her blisters begin to sting. The pain caused her to shout.

The two males were chatting. Sly turned to see Curane sitting by the waterside. "I knew it. She's having trouble with her feet." They turned back towards Curane, who was now ecstatic at the coldness of the water cooling her feet.

"Don't worry. I'll be fine in a minute."

Toska began to fumble in his carrier. He pulled out a tube of what looked like a soothing substance.

"Dry your feet, Curane, and I'll rub some of this on for you. It works wonders. You'll be able to run later." He laughed as Curane removed her feet from the water and began to dry between her toes gently, using a piece of cloth taken from Toska's medical supplies. He began to massage the watery mixture into her feet, and she felt a stinging sensation.

Sly was not impressed. He looked at Curane with disapproval and began to worry that she might not be able to make the trek. He suggested changing her footwear, but nothing else seemed suitable.

Curane began to lift herself up as Toska helped her to regain her balance. "I'm fine. I'll be OK now. Thanks." She pulled her arm away from Toska and linked arms with Slyster. Feeling grateful for the soothing of her new feet, she began to walk quickly.

"I know that Toska said you would be able to run, but hold on a minute, Curane. I can't keep up with you." Sly was slowing down. The effect of staying awake all night was now beginning to show.

"Come on, Sly, you will have to walk faster than this!" Curane shouted as she skipped on ahead. Sly was looking pale and decided to rest. As he lowered himself onto the ground, he cried out in pain. His body rolled into a ball, and his arms folded tightly beneath his chest.

He began to shout to Curane, who was wandering off into the distance, oblivious to what was happening behind. Toska heard the shouts and ran towards Sly, who was now breathing intensely. He loosened the neck of his shirt and lifted him onto his side. Sly had stopped breathing, and his chest was motionless. There was no pulse, and his lips had turned blue.

Curane had disappeared out of sight. Toska began to panic as he injected Sly with adrenaline and started to pump onto his chest with his hands. Sly was not responding. Toska carried on thumping, but to no avail.

He looked up to see Curane looking down at the motionless body below. He had not heard her approach. Tears had filled her eyes, and she knew that Sly was gone. "I tried everything, Curane, but nothing worked."

Curane knelt on the ground beside Sly and held his hand. She stared into his face, which felt cold when she pressed her mouth against it. She sobbed into his chest and held onto him like she never wanted to let go. Toska moved away to let Curane have her last moments alone with Sly. He felt awkward and didn't know what to do or say to help comfort her. He walked over to the edge of the stream, stared into the water, and watched the pebbles below the muddy trickle. He remembered the time when the stream was clear and fish were seen swimming towards the sea. The stream had become a grey slush.

Curane was still crying as Toska returned to see his new-found friend lying on the ground.

"Curane, there's nothing we can do now. I'm so sorry." He held out his hand to lift her up, and she grasped at it, pulling herself away from Sly. Toska held her in his arms, and she sobbed into his shoulder. He stroked her hair and wiped the tears from her face, but they wouldn't stop falling. Her body was shaking, and her face was swollen with sadness.

"What do we do now? I don't know where Sly was going. I don't know which friends he was going to see." Curane looked into Toska's eyes. She was frightened and felt cold and alone. "I don't know what I'm going to do now." She was confused and bewildered. "How am I going to go on now without Sly? I want Sly." She fell towards Sly, and Toska pulled her back.

"Curane, he's gone. We'll have to find somewhere to bury him."

"No, he's not being buried. Sly never wanted to be buried. He wanted to go into the ocean."

"Curane, the ocean is at least five miles away."

"Well, we'll carry him between us. It's what he wanted."

"Don't let me down now, Toska—not now when I need you most." Toska wasn't going to let her down. He was just thinking out loud.

They decided to spend the night by the stream. Tomorrow they would carry Sly towards the ocean.

CHAPTER 3

A STORM WAS BREWING. CURANE HAD COVERED SLY WITH HER sweater. She and Toska had placed him on two pieces of wood bound together by thin cord that Toska had found in his carrier. Curane was cold as she sat shivering beneath the trees, watching the weather change in the darkness of the night. The rain began to fall hard, and the stream was rising rapidly. Toska was quietly staring into the night, deep in thought. Curane didn't want to talk; she was glad Toska was silent for a few hours. It was too cold to sleep, and the sound of the moisture falling in a heavy downpour was something she would never forget.

As daylight approached, Toska began to gather his belongings together. "We must go now, Curane."

The rain had stopped, and the stream had turned into a copious flow.

Toska had an idea. He thought it might be easier if they walked downstream with Sly, instead of having to carry the corpse. Curane agreed, as they were already drenched from the night before. They lowered Slyster and themselves into the river and stood on either side of him, holding onto the wooden frame. The flow of the water went with them as they waded towards the ocean.

"Look, Toska, I can see the ocean."

As they approached the open space, they felt a strong current rush towards them. They let Sly go. He floated out with the current, and before long he had become a spot in the distance. They stood and watched him disappear into the horizon. Curane felt a chill go up her spine. She didn't cry but walked back towards the side of the stream and sat awhile. Toska sat beside her. They held hands in silence.

"We had better find some dry clothes, Curane." Toska proceeded to undo his carrier. He had carried it around his shoulders, and the weight of it had rubbed against his skin. He found some dry clothing and began to undress. He hung his wet clothes on a nearby bush to dry. Curane began to do the same. Toska began looking around. As he spotted something in the distance, he shouted over to Curane.

"Curane, look, there's an island over there. I wonder what it is?" He could see a building with antennas stretching up into the sky.

"It looks like some kind of communication centre. Come on, put your wet clothes back on, and let's swim over and have a look round."

Curane wasn't really interested. She was missing Sly and didn't really want to go anywhere. She frowned at Toska, who demanded she get dressed and come.

Curane unwillingly obliged. The two of them dived into the water, leaving their belongings behind. They swam towards the island and, once there, made their way into the building.

There was a room surrounded by electronic machines. They were minute in size with built-in monitors.

Curane and Toska continued into the next room to discover small tubes in a large Perspex cylinder. The room was surrounded with automated metallic storage cabinets, which were difficult to open without a power supply.

Toska stood on tiptoe, leant across, and peeped into the cylinder. "I don't believe it, Curane. There are organisms in these tubes."

Curane was confused. She had forgotten Toska had studied medical science.

"Well, they are not sperm or eggs. They are living matter."

Toska was beginning to get stimulated as he inspected them closely. "Curane, there are names and dates on these tubes."

The tubes were all lined up in rows of fifty. There must have been at least one thousand tubes. Like soldiers waiting to go to battle, they were all labelled and in alphabetical and chronological order.

He studied them like someone would study a book. He had never seen so many. The organisms lay dormant. There was no sign of life.

Whoever was controlling this project may have left in a hurry, and the matter had been neglected. The living matter which once survived in these tubes had stopped functioning.

Toska proceeded to open one of the automated metallic storage cabinets. It was locked, which infuriated him. He kicked it and pulled with force, but it wouldn't budge. Carrying on to the next available cabinet to see if it would open, with full speed, he was like something possessed.

"Toska, slow down." He had mostly been calm and in focus. Curane pulled his arm and turned him around to face her.

"Toska, what on earth are you doing?"

"I've never seen anything like it, Curane. It's all I've ever dreamed about.

To stumble across something like this, it's just amazing." "Why? What? Tell me."

"Look! All these cabinets must hold information about this experiment." "What experiment?"

"I'm not sure, Curane. Whatever it was involved people who had donated living matter, and that living matter was put into those tubes. It could be anything."

Curane was now deeply involved in Toska's conversation. She stared at him with her mouth open wide. She wanted to speak, but the words wouldn't come. She sat down on the floor beside the cabinet as Toska began to pace the floor. She was grieving for her Sly.

"I could go on forever, but there is a lot you would never understand, Curane. Things have happened that even I don't understand. When I was studying medical science, animals were used for medical research, but this looks like human tissue has been used."

He closed the automated metallic storage cabinet with his foot as he passed it, walking directly towards the tubes. The container shook, making a loud noise that echoed around the building. Toska had begun to inspect the tubes again. He was fascinated.

It was getting dark.

As the night was drawing in, Toska and Curane decided to swim ashore and then rest for the night. In the distance they could see the island. Tomorrow they would inspect the lab more closely.

CHAPTER 4

A S THE MORNING BROKE, THE LIGHT BEGAN TO SHINE THROUGH the clouds. Curane opened her eyes to brightness beyond belief. It wasn't the daylight but a shining object hovering above.

Feeling unbalanced, her body soared above the ground, higher and higher into the shinning bright light. She was being drawn into the large object, and suddenly her being was abducted into a large room surrounded by small people of an alien source.

They were approximately four feet tall with enormous heads and large ears. Their eyes were oval-shaped and black, filled with emptiness. She began to feel uneasy as they stared at her with disapproval. They began nodding their heads and touching her as if inspecting her body.

As she stood still, the beings left her and began to scurry around the room, collecting objects to examine her with.

Curane felt nervous. She knew that aliens existed, having seen them on monitors recorded from crafts, but she had never been this close to any before. They returned and started to prod her with sharp objects.

She began to bleed. The aliens took samples of her blood and poured it into a cylinder. They hurried her into a tunnel, and the light appeared again as she was transported back down to Toska, who was still sleeping soundly.

"Toska, wake up." She thumped him harshly with her fist. Toska moved with great speed.

"What are you doing?" "Let's go."

Curane headed off into the distance, away from the island they had visited the evening before.

"I thought we were going back?" He began to walk the other way.

"Toska!" shouted Curane. "I don't want to go back to the island. Let's just go."

"No way. I'm not leaving without some answers." "You won't find the answers in there."

Curane sat down and began to explain to Toska what had happened while he was sleeping. Toska didn't flinch. He began to nod his head and told Curane that the same thing had happened to him on more than one occasion. The thing is, he told her, that once the aliens get a grip, they don't let go, and you become a human guinea pig.

"They seem to collect blood for something. Who knows what for. Maybe they drink it. Maybe they are alien vampires."

Curane laughed.

"Curane, it's been going on for hundreds of years, maybe thousands. There are other worlds out there, lots of them, but each one is different.

"I think you are looking a bit pale. Here, have one of these."

Toska began to rummage into his carrier and brought out a small tablet. "It's glucose. It will give you energy. Just take your time with it. It's the last one."

Curane savoured the sweet taste. Her eyes slowly began to feel alive again.

She stared at Toska, who smiled with approval.

Curane now began to cooperate. Her mind was focusing on what was important. It was imperative that she learn more about this experiment.

"I'd better go and get some food; we can't go another day without eating," Toska said. "You stay here, Curane, and I'll have a walk around and see if there are any edible goods."

Curane wanted her Sly so much that the pain was hanging over her like some dark cloud that wouldn't go away. Oh, how she missed him.

On his return, Toska brought some fruit and dried leaves. They both sat on the ground with their backs against the tree and began to suck what they could out of the remains of the food.

Curane looked over to the island and thought about what was in that building. Tubes, containers, names, dates—what did it all mean?

The wind began to rustle the branches, and she knew another storm was brewing. The sky was grey, and the air was filled with smoke, which seemed to be a little weaker today as the wind was blowing it in all directions.

The antennas were swaying with the wind. There were seven in all. Curane counted them as she and Toska swam towards the island. It was cold, and they didn't have any dry clothing with them. It was all hanging on the tree trying to dry in the cold, damp, smoky air.

On entering the building and looking round, they both felt that things seemed different this time. They tried to dry themselves off with bits of paper.

Curane shivered. "I'm cold."

"It's freezing in here. I wonder if we can make some kind of heating." Curane looked around to see if there was anything she could turn into heat. "Hey, I've found some matches, some candles, a torch with no batteries, paper clips, a broken bulb, and paper—tons and tons of paper. We could do with some wood. Then I could light a fire in the far room in that old metal bin."

Toska left to find some wood. He came back with branches and bits of dry leaves. Curane made the fire while Toska went to find some thicker wood for later. Slyster came into her mind: his soft brown eyes, his laugh, his black hair, and his beautiful smile.

Toska returned with enough wood to keep the fire going for a day or so. Curane stood against the fire and dried herself the best she could. She rubbed her hands. Toska joined her.

"That's better."

Curane agreed and began to run her fingers through her hair to unknot it, as it was wet and tangled.

"You have nice hair," Toska said.

Curane smiled but didn't think her hair was particularly nice compared to Slyster's, whose hair was thick and curly.

"Where shall we start?" Curane asked.

"Not sure, but we can probably look into the storage cabinets over there." He pointed towards the other room and the cabinets he had struggled to open the day before.

Curane struggled to open them. Taking the paper clip, she uncurled it and prodded the hole of the cabinet to see if it would unlock. She tugged at the cabinet as she jammed the paper clip into the hole. The cabinet opened, and she fell back and lost her balance. It fell on top of her leg, and she screamed in pain. Toska flew across the room and lifted it from her.

Curane tried to raise herself up from the floor with the help of Toska, but the pain was crippling. She couldn't make it.

"I didn't think the whole thing would come tumbling down!" she shouted.

Toska gently placed her back down on the floor. "Let's have a look," he said. He stared at Curane's leg and gently pressed his finger against it. Curane screamed again.

"Looks like you are going to have some bruising tomorrow."

He soaked some paper in a bowl of dripping water that was in the back room under a tap that looked like it hadn't been turned on for years. He couldn't turn the tap, and the amount of water that dripped wasn't really enough to do the job.

Upon returning, he touched Curane's leg with the paper, and she sobbed with the pain.

"Is it broken?" she cried.

"No, I don't think so. Give it a few minutes, and then we will try to get you up again."

"Thanks, Tos. I'm sorry. I just didn't think." "It's OK."

As she sat upon the cold, hard floor, Curane began to play with her locket.

She twisted the chain between her fingers.

The locket was open. She looked at the photo of Sly and her.

Curane burst into tears again. Toska was beginning to feel as though he should have done this alone.

Her sobbing became uncontrollable. Toska wasn't in the mood for pity. He held her hand but didn't really know what else to do.

"Curane, you need to rest. Just make yourself as comfortable as possible."

She wedged herself against the wall and closed her eyes. Her leg was throbbing, and she wished she were under the tree. She felt safe there; plus, the ground was softer.

"I'm OK. I just need to close my eyes for a while. You carry on. I'll listen."

"The problem is that with these old automatics, they need electricity to open them properly, so we will have to use the paper clip and do it manually, which is going to take up a lot of time. But here we go."

Toska gently pulled at the cabinet, as it had closed again. It opened with ease.

"Wow, Curane, this looks interesting."

Toska flipped through the cabinet and then moved onto the next.

Curane began to feel faint and wished she had never come to the island.

Her head began to ache and her eyes narrowed, which disturbed her. "How's that leg?"

Curane felt dizzy. She saw two of Toska. Then her eyes closed, and she drifted into a deep sleep.

A man was running after her as she ran as fast as her legs would carry her. She came to a halt as there was no exit. She turned around and looked into the face of Sly. Her beloved was there next to her. He spoke to her in a small voice and told her not to be afraid. He said he would look after her and that she had no need to worry. It all seemed so real. She awoke to Toska stroking her head. She muttered the name Sly, wishing it was him.

"Curane, are you OK?"

Toska was leaning over her, looking into her pale blue eyes. "I'm sorry. I think I must have fainted."

Her leg was still painful. She began to lift herself up again. Toska was steadying her. "Take it easy."

"I'm OK. I think we should get back to the tree, Toska." "Will you be able to swim with that leg?"

"No, I don't think so. What was I thinking?"

"We'll have to sleep here. I think we should put some more wood on the fire."

Toska proceeded to stoke the fire. The flames soon began to roar, and the heat felt warm and cosy.

"Perhaps we should forget the tree and stay here for a while. We could make it habitable."

Curane wasn't too sure. She liked it under the tree. It reminded her of her childhood—days spent with Slyster and his parents.

Those days were gone forever.

"Yes, Toska, I think that would be a good idea. For a while at least." Toska was elated.

He studied the contents of the cabinets he had come across with intense scrutiny.

Curane was beginning to feel better as she tried to lift herself off the ground and balance herself against one of the other storage cabinets.

"Curane, what was Slyster's name?" "Slyster Lister Teape," she answered. "How old was he?" Toska asked curiously. "Twenty-five." She looked puzzled.

"Twenty-five? Curane, look. This tube has got 'Slyster Lister Teape' on it. It's empty; there's nothing in it. I don't know, maybe it's just a coincidence, but it seems a bit too much of a coincidence having the same name. And I'm sure that is a creation date."

"No! Sly was definitely produced from natural parents." Curane began to shake her head in disapproval.

"But how do you know, Curane?"

"I knew his parents. He looked like them." Curane was frowning. "Is that it, Curane? He looked like them?"

"Well, yes. And you could tell he had their characteristics."

"Curane, do you know what a database of information can do? If you feed it with the correct info, it can find the perfect match to what you are looking for."

"I know that, but Sly created? No, I don't think so." She began to hesitate and feel uncomfortable.

Toska had made a comment, but she did not want to discuss the matter any further.

Curane wasn't happy and didn't want to believe it could have been Sly in that tube.

"Think about it, Curane. Sly's mother and father wanted a replica of someone, or maybe just characteristics of themselves."

"You know, Toska, Sly is gone now, and I'm still grieving. And now you're telling me he may have come from that tube. Have you no feelings or consideration for how I must be feeling right now?"

Toska felt ashamed. He had built himself up into a frenzy. He had forgotten himself. "I'm sorry, Curane. I just wasn't thinking. I got carried away."

Curane accepted his apology.

They advanced into the far room at the rear of the building, Curane limping slightly and slowly behind. It contained more metal cabinets, unlocked. Toska began to rummage through the files quickly, hoping to find some kind of enlightenment. The files held records of persons over the age of eighteen with photographs, characteristics, and dates. There were files for both males and females, but Toska noticed something strange: they all had the same blood group, Rh null.

He shouted to Curane to come over. She appeared, looking pale and withdrawn.

"Curane, there are photographs and information on people. They all seem to have the same blood group—Rh null.

Curane began to look for herself. She went to the back of the file and began to look for the name Teape. It was there, with a photograph of Slyster Lister Teape. Rh null blood group. Black hair, brown eyes. It was most certainly Slyster. Prospective parents were listed as Lister Teape and Constance Teape. No other family was recorded.

Toska was back on track. His brain began to click into gear. Nothing was going to change his thought pattern.

"Curane, listen to me please." Toska had turned her around to face him. "Don't say anything, just listen."

She stared into Toska's eyes and was ready to listen to what he was about to say.

"When I was studying medical science, we had to use animals. Humans were not allowed for experimental purposes. I studied for three years, and I learnt how to create identical species by using the same organisms each time. "These cells in here may have been used more than once, which means there could be more than one. You see, Curane, some matches are popular, and different parents may ask for the same one. That is why you see so many people today who really do look alike. They favour particular genes and characteristics.

"Also, if you keep to the same blood group, it becomes simpler and easier.

Curane, creation has become far more advanced than people can imagine."

It was getting dark. Light was limited as Toska began to stoke the bin with wood. Curane made herself as comfy as possible.

The floor was hard, and they had limited clothing. They decided to lean on one another and fold into each other to keep warm.

Curane's leg was feeling better. Toska rubbed it with his cold hands as she jumped with unease. He laughed as she thumped his arm in retaliation.

"Toska, I think we should move on tomorrow." "Why?"

"I just feel as though we need to find the others. The New Polity, you know, friends of Sly's—we just need to move on. Forget the island and just, you know, move on."

"What about your leg?" "I'll be OK."

"Let's see how you feel in the morning." "OK."

The night was long. It was cold and uncomfortable. The floor was hard, and Curane's leg was troublesome.

CHAPTER 5

T HE MORNING BROKE. CURANE NUDGED TOSKA IN ORDER TO wake him. Her leg was feeling better and she wanted to move, but Toska was lying on her, snoring in a very annoying way. He awoke and moved over to one side. Curane managed to pull herself up. She could see the sun shining through one of the windows as she made her way outside.

She knew she could swim back from the island. The thought of doing so felt good. Toska appeared. They collected their things and returned to carry on with their journey to find the New Polity friends. They needed to help them organise a better world, as they knew they couldn't do it alone.

Curane hobbled along the best she could while Toska walked on in front of her. They were behind schedule now as they had spent so much time on the island. The time it would have taken them to reach Sly's friends had now become longer.

All Toska could think about was the lab and what he was leaving behind. Was it more important than finding the others? He supposed he could always go back again another time, but would it still be there? Would someone come and destroy it? Thoughts were going through his mind, and he tried to dismiss them and carry on. He turned round to look at Curane, who was slowly limping behind him, and he sat on the ground while she caught up.

Curane seated herself next to him. She rested. "What happens, Curane, when we find the others? What do we do then?"

"We form a body of people to fight against the officers and try to bring peace and harmony to the world again. That's what we do. That is what it's all about. We cannot be dictated by the officers. They are bad people. You know that."

"Yes, I know that."

"Come on, two more days max."

Curane managed to lift herself up as Toska held her arm. They carried on walking towards Crombie Mountain.

They walked for two days without sleep. The nights were long and cold. They had no visitors from an alien source, and things were beginning to look a little too quiet. They hadn't met or spoken to anyone along the way, and all they could see was the mountain in the distance, which seemed to be getting farther away.

They couldn't hear the ocean anymore, and the sound of the chanting and fires burning had now gone. There was a stillness and quietness Curane had felt before.

Curane felt unhappy. She was unhappy to be away from the place where she had lived with Sly. Now that he was gone, she didn't need to go back there. There was nothing there for her anymore. She missed him. Oh, how she missed him, but going back wouldn't help the pain go away. She wanted to forget about the island. It didn't matter whether Sly was conceived or created; he wasn't in her life anymore.

Toska was her new-found friend, and she enjoyed his company. They could never be lovers. She didn't want that. Not now, not ever. Sly was the only man for her, and anyone else just didn't fit the picture. She was still young, young enough to fall in love again, but that was far from her mind. Slyster had been her life and always would be.

Suddenly there was the sound of running water. A stream maybe. It was trickling along beside the road they were walking. The sound had broken the silence of dry footsteps. The water was clear, and one could see the small stones beneath the surface. It looked man-made, and it seemed to flow from beneath the mountain.

They could see the opening.

They were greeted with a loud voice echoing around the inside of the cave. Curane wasn't sure if this was the place Slyster had wanted them to go to, but within minutes the man introduced himself to the visitors, who were friends of Slyster's.

Groups of people were surrounding the inside of the cave. It was large enough to hold a gathering of maybe two thousand people.

In the centre there was a large fire burning with flames hovering up to the heights above. They seemed to dance as they hit the top.

People were surrounding the fire as if to keep warm. The light reflected from their faces with a warm glow.

For the first time in weeks, Curane felt warm inside. She smiled at Toska, who returned the look with approval.

Voices were loud but distinct enough to understand from a distance. The male greeter began to speak in tones of authority.

"We, the New Polity of Today, need to be strengthened. We cannot let the officers take over our world and destroy the spirit of our new-found freedom. The world needs to be built up with the spirit of the New Polity of Today, who stand for truth and righteousness. The officers are growing in numbers, and we need to increase our followers as we prepare to fight against our enemies. We cannot let them proceed with their ways, with which we do not agree. If we do, we will never be free. We must group together in numbers of fifty and prepare ourselves for battle."

Weapons were given freely to all. Toska felt uneasy.

"I don't wish to get involved in all this. It really isn't what I came here for."

Curane agreed. "No, me neither. I've had enough of fighting, and weapons aren't my best skill."

Toska stepped forward and proceeded to take control of the situation.

"I may not be a good warrior, but I know some of us are capable of self- defence without weapons. Not all officers have guns, but they are trained to kill at first sight. Some of us here today may have gone through the training programme of self-defence, whereas the officers haven't. I would feel it a weakness to use the weapons. And it would be in our best interests to have the officers join us as one."

The greeter nodded approvingly.

"It needs to be a peaceful future we are creating, and we need to start now."

The greeter approached Toska. Friendship signs were made. Hands were touched all round, and people of the New Polity were pleased with the gathering today. Tyler and Idle were spotted in the distance but disappeared from view.

The flames had died down, and the people of the New Polity began to depart from the cave.

Where would they go from here?

Curane didn't want to go back. Slyster was gone, and there was nothing to go back to.

Several groups of people were wandering around introducing themselves.

Tyler and Idle came over with added enthusiasm. "Greetings, Curane. Where's Sly?"

Curane looked at them with a saddened expression. "He's gone." "Gone where?"

"Taken to another world somewhere."

Her eyes began to fill up, and she sobbed again. Tyler looked at Idle with confusion.

"He took ill and passed on." "We sent him out to sea."

Toska introduced himself and briefed the two with information on the previous days whilst Tyler hugged Curane tightly.

It was time to go. The cave was now in darkness. The flame had died down, and there was no point in staying there, as it was light and warmer outside. The four ventured outside, Tyler with his arm still around Curane. The sun was shining, and the warmth felt good against their skin. They washed in the stream, which was cool and clear, for a long time. Curane suddenly felt fresh and clean. The gathering had gone well. It was time to put The New Polity of Today into practise.

CHAPTER 6

A GROUP OF YELLOWCOATS APPEARED FROM INSIDE THE CAVE. They had been at the gathering but were not dressed in their attire. The atmosphere became solemn.

The officers spoke with a tone that was not agreeable for the others to accept.

"We don't wish to abide by your rules. We didn't come here today to make peace. We came to tell you that we are going to become leaders of this new world and that you will do as we say."

The weapons they were holding were now being pointed in the direction of the foursome. The latter had no choice but to follow the instructions of the former.

"You must come with us."

They all began to walk back into the cave. It was dark and uninviting. The foursome were in front of the group of officers.

"Keep walking."

Crombie Mountain was known for its huge vast open space, where hidden tunnels had been explored by many. The sound of running water could be heard, and the air smelt damp. It was cold. Curane wished she could be back outside in the sunshine.

They carried on walking. Curane could see a small light in the distance.

She thought it might be a way out of this dark, dismal place.

It was. As they approached it, the light became brighter and the hole became larger.

They all ventured into the open again, with the officers behind. Toska turned round. "Where are you taking us?"

The sun was beating down, and the light shone into his eyes, so he wasn't able to see the officers without feeling a blinding pain.

Their yellow uniforms were shining brightly and he could see they were still pointing their weapons at them.

"Just keep going."

They walked along a path surrounded by trees, the sun burning on their backs through their clothing. It was getting hot, hotter than usual for the time of year. The seasons had changed dramatically over the last ten years, and the grass was beginning to get very dry with the heat, even after all the rain of the previous days.

Curane tripped, and her shoe came off her foot as she stumbled to the ground.

Tyler bent down to help her back to her feet, and two yellowcoats approached with caution.

Tyler let go off Curane and swung round towards the yellowcoats as Tyler and Idle joined in to retrieve the weapons the officers were holding.

There was a scuffle, and the weapons were thrown towards the trees. As Tyler ran towards them and picked them up, the others began to show violence towards one another.

Tyler's voice bellowed above the trees: "*Stop*. This isn't what we were planning. We were all supposed to be working together."

He pointed the weapon at the yellowcoats and asked them to move to one side, pointing the gun in the direction he wanted them to go.

They obeyed.

"Turn around and go back the way we came."

The yellowcoats obeyed and walked quickly towards the opening of the mountain. They all proceeded to go through to the other side.

They decided it was time to go home. Toska would visit the island again as they were passing that way. They would have to take the Yellow coats with them.

Suddenly it dawned upon Curane that life back there was probably going to be different, but she would have to accept it. Where else was there to go?

She wanted to go home.

Toska could see the antennas in the distance.

The group followed Toska like a flock of young sheep would follow their mother. He was determined to understand what had been happening in the lab.

They made their way towards the island. Toska thought it would be better if he went onto it alone.

He suggested to Curane that she walk ahead with the others while he visited the island alone. She agreed, as she wasn't really interested in the outcome. Slyster was never away from her thoughts, but she didn't want to get involved in something she didn't really understand. And she wanted to get back home as quickly as possible.

She knew she would be safe with Idle and Tyler and the yellowcoats, who had been overzealous in their friendship.

They set off towards home.

CHAPTER 7

OSKA SWAM TOWARDS THE ISLAND.

On entering the building, he felt the cold air but was more concerned that someone may have been there after he and Curane had left.

Cabinets were left open, and samples had been removed from the trays.

There were fewer. Maybe half had been taken.

He looked for Slyster's information again, only this time it wasn't there.

There was nothing on Slyster Lister Teape. Toska's project was doomed.

He decided to leave quickly. He began to swim towards the bank and catch up with the others.

Curane was standing on the bank, waving. He could see her in the distance.

He wondered why she wasn't with the others. "Toska!" she shouted.

He swam faster. He could see something was bothering her. He pulled himself onto the bank as Curane ran over to him.

"It's Idle and Tyler. They have been attacked by the yellowcoats. They are dead, Toska. I managed to get away. I just ran as fast as I could. What are we going to do, Toska?"

Toska was concerned. Curane could have been attacked too. He decided he wasn't going to leave her side again until they returned home.

"Curane, I'm sorry. I shouldn't have left you alone with the others. Thank goodness you are okay."

Curane was shivering. Toska was standing in his wet clothes. There was nothing either of them could do.

They sat on the ground, trying to think of what the next step was going to be.

"We could swim back to the lab and stay there for the night." The darkness was drawing in.

Toska wasn't too sure about that. There had been a disturbance, and he wasn't too sure if it would be safe. "No, perhaps not," he told Curane. She didn't need to know anything more.

Toska stripped off his clothes, trying to hide as much of his body as possible. Curane had turned her back towards him. She passed him her top so he was able to cover himself. Toska hung his wet clothes to dry.

They both sat under the tree and huddled up together.

"I feel like we have gone round in circles," she said to him. "We've wasted all our time coming here."

"Lost two good friends, and what for? "*Nothing!*" she shouted.

Curane was beginning to feel exhausted. She closed her eyes and went to sleep. Toska wasn't far behind.

A light appeared from the top of the trees.

Curane and Toska were taken into a craft and were together inside some unknown area.

Small people were running around as they grabbed Curane and Toska. They laid them down onto a cold slab. They prodded and again took blood from both of them.

Their faces were familiar yet unknown.

Toska and Curane were then shuttled into another room, where a being of larger statue began to inspect their hair, nails, and ears. It was all very quick.

They were then taken back down to the tree. A beam of light lowered them to the ground.

They sat and looked at each other in awe.

"So it looks like I will be leaving you soon," said Toska. Curane began to sob.

"I can't control that. One day I'll be gone, taken to another world and away forever."

Curane tried to laugh it off between her tears.

"Yes, I'll wake up one morning and watch you disappear into the sky through a ray of light," Curane told him.

"They might take me while you're asleep," he said. They both giggled.

"Come on, let's get out of here. This place is giving me the creeps." Toska pulled Curane up from the ground. He was up and ready to go.

"There is something not quite right about this place. I need to get away now."

Curane began to follow him, even though he wasn't properly dressed. She could now see his long, skinny legs.

They passed Idle and Tyler, who were lying in the long grass. Curane stopped to look at her lifeless friends. How on earth had things gotten this bad?

They had all journeyed to find friends who could begin the New Polity of Today . She wondered where all the others were who had met at Crombie Mountain.

Toska and Curane walked through the night. As the sun rose, they were in need of a rest.

There was the sound of voices in the distance. Echoes of familiarity beckoned.

They listened for a few minutes and decided that the way they would go would be in the direction of those voices. It seemed to be the New Polity discussing their new-found freedom.

Curane followed Toska, who was still showing his spindly legs and looking in a state of undress. They walked through the trees and towards the voices, passing a vast amount of water on either side of the trodden path.

They were with the Yellow Peril, the two who had just destroyed Idle and Tyler. They all had been discussing the future.

At great speed Toska ran at the yellowcoats. He rammed into them, head down, and with great force separated the two of them.

"These two have just destroyed two of my friends!" he bellowed.

"Do not listen to a word they are saying, as they do not come in peace."

The others stood in awe. Not knowing what to do, they stared at one another.

"They are not peacemakers."

The Yellow coats began to run towards the trees. The others ran after them into the woods.

Toska and Curane stayed where they were, and within minutes everyone had returned, all except the two yellowcoats.

"They got away," said a very tall man wearing a garment of leather and black boots to match.

There must have been at least twelve of them conspiring and debating as to what was going to happen next.

"Come over here," he said to Curane and Toska. "Sit with us."

They all sat on the ground and formed a circle, as it was easier to engage in conversation in that position.

The tall man seemed to be the ringleader. He began to speak.

"We have met today to discuss the New Polity of Today, and we have all agreed that we don't want to accept the officers or Yellow Peril or Yellow coats—whatever you wish to call them—as members. We cannot trust them. It was wrong of us to even think that the two who came along were going to befriend us. So we will now agree that they must be destroyed on sight. All in favour, raise your hand."

All hands were raised.

Curane and Toska had raised their hands too, as Toska had now decided that this was the right approach.

The man in leather stood and made a sign with both hands that meant peace unto all.

Everyone copied him.

"Also we agreed this morning on the people who are going to stay here and start a New Polity of Today community by building huts for us to live in. We decided to begin straight-away by chopping down the trees. We agreed that help would be needed all round and that those that don't wish to be here need to go now. We haven't started yet, so come on, let's get a move on."

Curane looked at Toska, who looked at Curane.

She nodded her head in approval. She could see that Toska approved too. "We have tools, clothes, food, and plenty of water."

The area was ideal.

They all started to choose their equipment. It wasn't long before axes were being swung and saws were set into motion.

Trees were coming down for fun, and men were starting to join the logs together with pieces of leather that had been cut into strips of different lengths. Leather was in abundance.

Roofs were going to be made from roofing material like reeds or straw, something that was used centuries ago and was now becoming popular with the new climate that had begun to take shape.

Tools had been made, and ladders had to be runged.

The New Polity of Today community was beginning to take shape.

CHAPTER 8

CURANE WAS BEGINNING TO FEEL NORMAL AGAIN. Slyster was always in her mind, but she knew that things had to change. She would now have to begin her life again, without him, and what better way than to start again amongst a new community with new people whom she would get to know and who wanted the same things as she did?

Self-reliance was needed, and the New Polity of Today were on track.

Within weeks the huts were up. Roofs had been attached, and the weather had kept dry. Equipment had been made, and prosperity for growing food was being established in the area. Perishable food items were still available for all, but fresh crops had been planted and were taking form.

Things were good. Curane and Toska had made new friends and were looking happier and healthier.

Horses and carts were used to transport heavy items. Sleeping arrangements had the males and females in separate huts unless couples were together as one.

The New Polity of Today were increasing in number. Each day people arrived, and more huts were built.

The Yellow Peril were nowhere in sight.

There was no heating source. The winters had become warmer, so there was no need for excess heating. The thatched roofing kept the heat in, and the beds and seating areas were made from the leftover wood and leather.

Bathing was done at the pools surrounding the area, males on one side and females on the other.

There was no sign of any children. People had become aware of life's changes and as a result weren't willing to bring children into the world as it now was. There was a sense that maybe now things could change for the better. It was going to take a long time, but maybe this was the start of a new world.

Building the huts was ongoing as more and more people came to join the community. There was no disturbances from rival gangs or the Yellow Peril. Peace was beginning to take shape, and Curane and Toska were starting to enjoy their new surroundings.

Toska often thought about going back to the building with the antennas just to see if there was anything more he could find out. There must be something more that would intrigue him, but he wasn't sure what. It wasn't too far away, and the thought was never far from his mind. He knew one day soon he was going to return. He would take Curane with him.

The busyness of the compound kept everyone alive with the spirit of a happier future.

New beginnings.

Then one evening while everyone was sleeping, a loud humming noise was heard coming from above the compound. It was loud enough to wake everyone up. Everyone ventured outside, where a bright light shone down from above.

A voice spoke, asking everyone to leave the compound. If they didn't do as requested, they would be exterminated.

It was the Yellow Peril. They were back.

No one moved, as they were not in a hurry to leave after all the hard work they had done.

The Yellow Peril were hovering above in a small vehicle with rotating blades.

"Please leave this area now, or you will be exterminated." Nobody moved.

Flames of fire came down from above and landed on the huts and surrounding areas. In no time they were ablaze. The New Polity of

Today people ran from their homes. Some dived into the water, while others just ran towards the trees.

Curane and Toska managed to find one another. Together they ran towards the water. Fire was surrounding their very beings. They both dived into the water and swam towards the other side of the lake, away from the flames that were being thrust around them. There was nothing they could do.

They stopped to look back and saw that the whole compound was ablaze.

The sky had lit up like an explosion of fireworks.

They dragged themselves out of the water and stared at the brightness of the sky. Another fateful day. Would it ever stop?

CHAPTER 9

Toska and Curane had no choice now. They had to move, but where to this time?

"Curane, come back to the island with me. I really need to have another look."

Curane wasn't going anywhere fast. She took Toska's hand, and he led her towards the island.

This time, once they got there, they noticed a canoe hidden behind the trees. The paddles were still inside. They decided to use the canoe to their advantage.

Toska paddled away as they went towards the island. They both wondered whom the canoe belonged to or whether it had just been abandoned. Either way, it came in useful.

They tied it up outside the building. Entering quietly, they had a feeling that something just wasn't quite right. The main door had been left ajar. They could see storage containers had been left open. Some had been ransacked.

Toska knew that someone had been back since his last visit.

He wandered around with Curane. She was closely behind him, holding firmly onto his arm.

There was a stillness in the air, a quietness of just the two of them breathing. Slowly they tiptoed around. There was no one there.

"I think we can safely say we are alone."

Curane looked at Toska as they began to find evidence of what had been kept in one of the metallic storage cabinets.

Slyster's records were gone. That was a certainty.

Toska fumbled through the cabinet that was nearest the door. It had been tampered with and files were missing, but he managed to scan through the ones that remained. He found one which caught his interest. It was labelled "Savion Inkling", the same name as his father.

He studied it carefully. Same name, same date of birth, same face. Yes, it was definitely him.

Blood type, Rh factor, same as Toska's.

"Curane, there's a file here. It's all about my father." "Are you sure?"

"Yes, it's him." "What does it say?"

"Savion Inkling donated living tissue on his death for research into living organisms to be used for the purpose of creating other human beings from micro organisms."

"Creating other human beings?" Curane was puzzled.

"That's what was in those cylinders. Living tissue for the creation of other human beings."

Curane was frowning.

"What about Slyster then? He had a file, and there was a cylinder with his name on it. He hadn't donated any living tissue."

"No. That might have been something different!" "Creation of other human beings!"

Toska frowned and looked at Curane in a disturbed manner.

"Another human being created from my father's living tissue. That could mean that there is someone out there who is exactly the same as my father!"

"He might not look like him though. I mean, would they have the same features?"

"Maybe not."

Curane thought for a while. She had come to terms with the fact that this project was now worth being interested in and with the possibility that Slyster could have been created from his own father's living tissue, but she wasn't sure how or why.

"Where do we go from here, Toska?" "I just don't know|"

The dawning day broke.

Toska and Curane had spent hours going through the cabinets. Exhausted, they slept on the floor of the building. Both were too tired to rise. They slept most of the day.

Curane dreamt about Slyster again. He was still running.

Toska was snoring loudly as Curane began to awake from her sleep. Looking over at Toska, she thought he looked rather young for his age.

She was still wearing the necklace Slyster had bought her and the ring Toska had given her with the blue sapphire stone. She thought how nice it would be to have some nice clean clothes and shoes, as the ones she was wearing were worn and beaten.

Curane pulled herself up from the floor and ventured outside, thinking about the night before and all that she and Toska had accomplished. She thought of how they had spoken of living tissue and microorganisms and DNA projects that had taken place over the years.

The canoe was still there, tied up in the bushes.

They weren't going anywhere for a while, as neither of them had the inclination or strength to rush off. Besides, there was too much research to do. More information was needed on this project.

Having had to abandon their new community, and having had nowhere else to go now other than back to where they had come from, Curane and Toska had inevitably ended up here.

Curane thought about the project. She knew that people could be cloned from various matter taken from parents or other humans, but creation was a different mindset. If scientists could create humans from cells taken from other humans—but notably they all had to have the same blood group—what was it all about?

She knew blood groups were variably different and that some respond to treatment better than others. And some types are not to be mixed with others as it weakens the immune system.

Curane was staring into the water, dreaming of Slyster. He was never far from her mind. Thoughts of their time together growing up as youngsters, and of being there for one another always, began to cause her eyes to fill with tears.

Thinking about him was something she did constantly, but this morning seemed to be a very emotional moment for her. As the tears came down her cheeks, she wiped them away with the back of her hand.

Curane sobbed quietly. It made her feel better. It was a release of emotion that had built up these last few days.

Toska appeared from nowhere as she composed herself. Curane didn't want Toska to know she was upset again.

The morning sky was bright blue with a warm feeling in the atmosphere. The breeze was light, and it looked to be a good day for canoeing down the river, the river that flowed to the sea where Slyster had gone all those weeks ago.

CHAPTER 10

THE THOUGHT OF CANOEING ENTERED CURANE'S MIND.

"Shall we have a canoe down the river? It's such a lovely day. We can always come back again?"

Toska frowned slightly, but she could see he was thinking it might be a good idea.

"Yes, let's," was his reply.

They tidied up inside and then readied the canoe, stepping into it carefully so as to not upset it.

Toska was the one with the paddle. Curane was relaxing, watching him struggle to set off. She decided to paddle with him as she took the other paddle.

The water was looking murky, and there was no sign of any life.

They began to paddle slowly away from the building with the antennas.

It must have been a functioning laboratory at some time, as all the signs were there—and not very long ago too.

The sun was coming up on the horizon. As they slowly ventured towards the sea, Curane felt a feeling of relaxation. It was good to just get away from the aftermath.

They carried on rowing. Conversation was not high on the agenda. Trees were on either side of the river, which had a very slow current flow.

There were no birds or animals of any sort. Fish had disappeared over time because of the poisoning of the riverbeds from humankind's waste. The sea was so polluted that the fish couldn't survive in the waters. Oceans were now larger because of climate change, but still pollution was rife. All Curane could see was the murky water underneath.

They began to paddle slightly faster as the sky became a dark grey. Rain clouds were forming, and it looked like a storm was brewing.

They began to paddle towards the trees in case they needed shelter. Suddenly the river began to swirl, and the canoe began spinning slowly.

Curane lost her paddle as the canoe tipped to one side. Both she and Toska ended up in the water.

Trying to swim in the middle of a whirlpool was difficult. The water was spinning as Curane and Toska were being sucked into a giant hole. Down they went into the hole, their bodies swirling into a vast emptiness of nothing. Spinning and spinning, they fell into something like unconsciousness, their bodies lifeless and uncontrollable.

Suddenly a beam of light shone through the water, lifting them out and onto the side of the river. There they were left in a state of deep sleep.

The rain was falling heavily onto the lifeless bodies, catching the leaves of the trees, which had turned a bright yellow. The storm was now in full force. Lightning was glowing and striking between the trees and, with full force, returning from the ground and travelling upwards, towards the sky above.

The thunder clapped, followed by more strikes of lightning, the rain falling continuously in a heavy downpour.

Curane and Toska lay motionless on the bank of the river as the black clouds hurried by, followed by more strikes and thunderclaps. A severe thunderstorm was imminent. The canoe had long gone.

A light suddenly appeared from a small gap between the trees. It shone upon Curane and Toska as if to greet them with a warm glow. It trickled across their bodies, and as if scanning for something, it proceeded back and forth. The light began to rotate around them as if searching for signs of life. Or was it giving them life?

The light formed a round shape as Toska and Curane disappeared into a sphere which gently lifted and returned to the small gap in the trees. It slowly lifted itself into the clouds and shot into the distance. It was now nowhere in sight of earth.

The rain stopped. The storm had finished its severity, and the sun began to come forth and shine.

Prod, prod, prod.

Curane and Toska were now aboard a craft again, only this time they were together and lifeless.

Prod, prod, prod.

Small people with oval-shaped eyes were scurrying around.

Instruments were prodding the humans who were lying dormant in the vicinity of their abode.

Noises were heard coming from the aliens bodies as they spoke their native tongue.

Curane and Toska were not breathing or moving. They lay still upon the table that was prominent in the craft. Two small beings dressed in white were prodding their bodies with a metal rod. These beings wrapped Toska and Curane separately in a roll of foil each and placed their bodies together underneath a long glass panel that produced heat from a mirror image. They began to stir. Both Toska and Curane were being revived, brought back to life. The process was working.

They opened their eyes to the sight of the mirror image of themselves, not knowing where they were or who it was that had brought them to this place. The last thing they remembered was being in the canoe.

They couldn't speak. Their lips were blue, and the blood had only just started to circulate in their bodies. They were unable to move as they had been fixed to the table.

A sharp instrument was inserted into Curane's arm. Unsure of what was happening, she looked over to Toska. He was staring into the mirror.

"Toska."

Curane spoke, her mouth feeling dry and swollen.

She could feel the sharp instrument in her arm as the beings were feeding something into her body. It made her feel alive, and she began to breathe again, her chest slowly rising and falling.

Toska was still staring into the mirror, not moving.

The other small being dressed in white began to insert a sharp instrument into Toska's arm. He responded quickly and looked over to Curane.

They made eye contact as they forced a smile, not really knowing what was happening or what was going to happen. The small beings in white were attaching another instrument to Toska's and Curane's bodies. This time it was inserted into the palms of their hands.

Curane flinched as the pain was unbearable. She wanted to hit out but was unable to move. She could see into the eyes of her intruder. They were brown and oval-shaped with large pupils. The creature was dressed in a white robe and hooded headdress, the robe covering most of its body.

Toska flinched also. He wondered why the beings would insert a rod into the palm of the hand, as it was such an unusual place to inject, but then again he and Curane were in an unusual place. This wasn't home; it was somewhere they hadn't known before. It was a place he had only dreamed about and wasn't sure it existed until after his first abduction. It was a place people only talked about, people who had visited for only a few moments and then were taken back home. Today was real.

Today was different. Curane was beginning to feel that these persons were interested in more than just people. They were interested in Curane and Toska.

Curane was beginning to feel awake—awake to the extent that she could do anything within her power.

Toska wasn't responding as quickly. He was still sleepy and was unaware of the other being entering the room. This one was taller than the other two. He was dressed the same but seemed to be older somehow. His skin was different; it was aged and slightly wrinkled.

The other two beings left, and the taller one flicked a switch, which gave Curane the freedom to move.

She stretched her whole body as the being went over to Toska, who was now beginning to look awake again. He too was now able to move.

Suddenly the mirror image flashed, and Curane and Toska were transported back to the stream amongst the trees, the light carrying them to the allocated place. They were here again, only this time with no canoe and in a spot they weren't familiar with.

They pulled themselves onto their feet and hugged one another, both feeling vulnerable and startled as to what had happened.

49

CHAPTER 11

"**I** NEED TO GO HOME. I NEED TO GO HOME. I NEED TO GO home."

Curane wanted to be home again. This time she hadn't any idea which way they would have to go. "Toska, I want to go home."

She knew Slyster wasn't going to be there, or his parents. She knew she would be alone. Maybe Toska would stay with her. Perhaps she should ask him now. Yes, that's what she would do. After all, he had been her companion most of the time since Slyster had passed. What should she do? Ask him now!

"Toska, would you take me home, please? I don't know the way. I haven't any idea where we are, but I need to go home. And once we get there, I would like you to stay with me."

"Sure, Curane. I think I can get my bearings. If we follow the stream towards north we should be going in the right direction, but I will be able to tell more when the sun rises in the morning. So maybe we should get some sleep, and then in the morning we will set off for home. I need to be sure we are going the right way, and I can't tell till sunrise."

They snuggled up under the trees and wrapped their arms around one another. Curane felt safe with Toska. He had been there for her since Slyster had passed, and now she accepted Toska as more than a friend. He was now her companion, and they would be together. He brushed her hair away from her forehead and kissed it softly.

They slept soundly in each other's arms until the morning sun rose.

The sun rises in the east and sets in the west. They needed to travel north towards home.

They woke up fairly early. Fortunately, the sun was blazing down.

They walked downstream, knowing that they would eventually come to a crossing, enabling them to choose a direction.

They walked for hours. The heat was becoming unbearable. Curane removed some excess clothing, which she carried wrapped around her waist. She was looking forward to seeing her old place again.

Several yellowcoats could be seen in the distance as they headed in Curane and Toska's direction. Toska wondered if they would still be aggressive towards them, as time had passed since they'd last made contact. And the plan was that they all were to get together to form the New Polity of Today even though the yellowcoats had just destroyed the new community. What if it was them?

Friend or foe?

Toska and Curane were both unsure, but they carried on walking. They knew that they would soon find out. And there wasn't anything else they could do other than run away again into the trees.

The Yellow Peril spotted Curane and Toska and began to walk towards them. Within no time at all, they had all congregated together, and all was well. The yellowcoats smiles spoke kind thoughts as they held out their hands to greet Curane and Toska. Toska asked them if they knew which way they should go to get back to where Curane and Slyster had lived. Did these people want to travel with them? Perhaps they could start again from where they'd first begun. They could build up the New Polity from there. At least they would have a roof over their heads.

What if others had moved in and had taken over their belongings? The Yellow Peril pointed them in the right direction. They didn't want to accompany Toska and Curane, as they were looking for others of their own kind, but they said they were planning on joining them once they met up with the others.

Curane and Toska set off in the direction the yellowcoats had indicated. They decided to hold hands along the way. It was comforting for both of them.

They walked through the night and for another day, seeing more people along the way.

CHAPTER 12

T HERE IT WAS, THE PERSPEX TOWER THAT TYLER HAD LIVED IN for those two years.

"Toska, I can see it. Tyler's tower." Only this time it was lit up like a beacon. Someone must be living there.

They made their way towards Curane and Slyster's place. It was just as it was when they'd left. Nothing had changed.

Curane smiled as she looked around at her and Slyster's belongings. She felt happy to be home again. She lay on the feathered bed, and Toska lay with her.

From her reclining position, Curane could see the tower through the window. The light was shining into their room. In the morning they would go and investigate to determine who was now living in Tyler's tower.

It was good to be home and to wake up in her own bed, although it wasn't easy to be surrounded by Slyster's items. Maybe Toska could go through them and dispose of them. There wasn't anything Curane wanted, but maybe Toska could make use of some of the items. They were men's things, small pocketknives and torches; tools and clothes; bags; and items Curane had bought Slyster over the years.

Curane wandered into the bathroom. It was small but comfortable enough to have a shower. Her perfumes and toiletries were still there, and she now realised how much she had missed them, the comforts of home. She showered and found some nice clean clothes, which were now too big as she had become smaller in size.

Toska was still sleeping. Curane decided to go over to the tower to see who was living there.

She ventured outside. Everything was the same as it was when she'd left.

Little had changed. The entrance to the tower was open. She climbed the stairs to the top. There was no one to be seen. She began to wonder how the power had been sustained as during the night the tower was alight.

She turned the power on, and nothing happened. There was no power and Curane had expected to have some form of connection.

Nothing had been altered from the time she was last there. There was no sign of anyone having been there or any changes to the room plan. The old monitors were still there that Idle had tried to fix and connect to the ones he had brought over to her house.

Curane left and wandered back to her place.

Toska had awakened and was looking out of the window, probably looking for her.

"I'm here, Toska."

She walked over to him. His arms were outstretched. They hugged each other tightly, and Curane felt safe and secure, something she hadn't felt in a long time.

"I need to say something, Toska." "Well, say it then!"

"Don't ever leave me!"

He had no intention of leaving her. He hugged her even tighter.

"Toska, I went over to the tower to see who was living there. There was no sign of anybody even having been in it. Also, the power wasn't working. I can't understand how it was lit up last night when there is no communication with any energy supply whatsoever."

Toska frowned. Curane could see that he was thinking. She kept quiet for a few minutes.

"Toska?"

He stared out of the window, looking in the direction of the tower. "Perhaps the power was working until today, and maybe it just went off today."

Curane thought that was probably the only logical explanation. She wandered over to the window to have another look.

Tyler's tower. He had planned and built it himself. She had watched him work very hard. It had to be the way he wanted it. He was so proud of his engineering skills that he defeated everything that had come his way to stop it from being built. Now it was empty, and Tyler was gone, along with Slyster.

Toska was thinking again. "Perhaps we should move into the tower. Then we would be able to see what is happening, and it may be warmer. There is only one window in here, and it's not very warm. The tower must be warmer.

"Do you agree?"

Curane wasn't sure. She was nodding her head. It seemed like a good idea, but she had to think about it.

"You haven't been inside it yet."

"I know, but I can see it's got to be better than here!" "Yes, Toska, but there is no light."

"There is less light in here."

The more Toska thought about it, the more it made sense.

"Curane, I can make light. All I need is some plastic bottles filled with water and some sunshine. It's very simple really."

Toska was using his science skills again. He had it all worked out in his mind that he was going to find some plastic bottles, which were very rare today. Most of the plastic items had been turned into products to make a better environment, and there wasn't any need anymore for such a material.

Where would they find some plastic bottles?

They decided to go out and have a look in the buildings that surrounded their environment. Shops and stores had once been alive in the vicinity but were now desolate.

Perhaps they would find some plastic bottles in the stores. They ventured in. There were damaged goods everywhere.

People had just ransacked the store. Food was literally thrown around on the shelves and floor. It was a breeding place for rats.

Curane and Toska looked in the rear of the building. It was in the same condition as the front. Curane remembered how she used to buy her food from here. It was only five years ago.

Time had taken its toll on her and Slyster. It now felt like yesterday since they'd been happy together.

Curane spotted some bottles in the corner. It was dark, and she and Toska were unable to see.

"Toska, over there in the corner!"

Toska proceeded over to the corner of the building. Curane was right: there were lots of plastic bottles filled with rapeseed oil. He placed them into a box and carried them over to the tower.

Curane had followed him.

He emptied the oil into a bowl and filled each bottle with water. He took the bottles to the top of the tower, where he placed each one inside a hole for the sunlight to solar-power them. He was pleased with his effort.

Curane looked around and thought about what Toska had said regarding moving in.

"Right. Let's do it!" Curane was happy now that she knew Toska had the right idea.

After spending the day sorting things and carrying them from one abode to the other, they began to settle down. They were now in their new place. Curane felt better about it now, knowing that it was hers and Toska's.

She would never forget Slyster, but somehow she had to move on, and meeting Toska and planning things with him helped her to do that. He was now her new love.

She was still wearing his ring and Slyster's locket.

CHAPTER 13

THEIR NEW HOME WAS NOW TAKING SHAPE. TOSKA HAD PUT SO much into the place. Curane helped by adding some luxury items. Life was beginning to improve once more.

The New Polity of Today was beginning to grow. Curane and Toska used the tower as their headquarters. The Yellow Peril had taken sides, and peace and harmony was developing in a very strong way.

People were happier. Children were being born into this new society and were welcomed by all. Curane and Toska even talked about having children, but none had come forth. Their love for one another grew. Their time spent together was very precious.

People were helping to create this new environment, growing food, making water wells, and improving buildings—all things that needed to be done to help build up this new world.

There was no leader.

Everyone was equal. The New Polity of Today was run by a group of people, including Curane and Toska, who were willing to work hard and make things happen. It was working well. Everyone was cooperating.

People were willing to use their time and energy to improve the welfare and state of this community. What was happening outside their community was unknown, as they still hadn't had any communication with the outside world.

All means of communication had been destroyed. The artificial satellites were now abandoned and unused as there was no power to sustain them. Occasionally one would fall from the sky, and people would just be happy that they hadn't landed on them or their property.

The World Wide Web had been corrupted with numerous hackers to the point of unusability. There was no way of communicating other than through direct contact.

The tower consisted of three floors, the top floor being the brightest as the solar-powered bottles brought plenty of light into the room. This was where Curane and Toska spent most of their time when indoors.

The second floor consisted of the bathroom and their sleeping quarters, and the ground floor was the entrance and also the meeting area for the gatherings of the New Polity.

Each floor was separated by a spiral staircase with thirty Perspex steps.

The meetings were held once a week. The New Polity of Today was growing in numbers. Toska conducted the meetings, whilst others were very willing to share their thoughts. New ideas were welcomed by all.

The human body needs food and water to survive. A person can go more than three weeks without food, but water is a different story. Humans can only go three to four days without it.

How to purify water and make sure it was suitable for drinking was high on the agenda. How to grow food was also high on the list, as people were so used to getting their food from the shops and stores. No one really grew anything anymore.

People of the New Polity were willing to share their skills. Basic courses were on the agenda.

This new community was beginning to take shape, and all was well. Ideas were needed to produce energy, and many ideas were coming in. Water power was a must as the river wasn't too far away.

Windmills were on the agenda for pumping water, grinding grain or spices, and generating power.

Basically the people were going back to the basic style of living.

The river's current had become strong as the rain had fallen in heavy downpours of late.

The windmill was now finished, and the wind and the strength of the river's current had increased the speed of the rotating blades.

Toska was impressed with his mechanical toy. He spent most days in the windmill making sure it was working and generating the power that was needed for a new electricity supply.

Curane spent a lot of her time with the others, both male and female, at the tower, planning and organising things that still needed attending to.

Children were happier. They seemed to enjoy the great outdoors, something they hadn't been used too. One of the adults had tied a rope to a tree and attached a tyre to it so the children were able to swing across the river on it. They were screaming with delight.

Huts were built around the tower so that the tower was a central base for everyone. That way Curane and Toska could keep an eye on things from the tower if needed.

The huts were made of clay and straw.

The place was turning into a small village. More people were arriving and wanting to settle and join the new community.

This time there was a better chance of it working as the yellowcoats were now gone or reformed.

Curane had gone to see Toska at the windmill. She was wearing her hair up and had found some clothes that she hadn't worn in a while. Her blonde ponytail was bobbing up and down. In her blue denim jeans, she ran over to the windmill.

Toska was mending the sails on the windmill; they had become worn from the rain and the wind. He greeted Curane with a large smile. He was happy to see her as they had spent far too much time away from each other. He came down to greet her, picking her up and swinging her round in his powerful arms.

She laughed and felt happy that they were together. "So to what do I owe this pleasure?"

Curane smiled. "I thought we could spend some time together. I was beginning to forget what you look like."

Toska invited her into the windmill.

It was cold and dark and very uninviting. There was a staircase to the top, and you could see outside through the tiny windows.

"Curane, I've been working on something for you. It's a surprise. I've nearly finished it. I hope you will like it."

Her eyes opened wider than ever. She was really interested in what this surprise was going to be.

"I love surprises!"

Toska had been working on a bicycle. All that was left to do was to attach the brakes and tighten them up. The bike was bright red with a bell and basket at the front.

Curane squealed with glee. She loved it!

Quickly jumping onto the seat, she balanced herself on the bicycle with one foot on the ground. It was perfect.

"Toska, that's what you've been doing all this time? I am amazed."

She took the cycle outside, knowing it had no brakes, and cycled a short distance and back again.

"When will it be finished?"

Toska smiled. He was pleased she liked it so much and decided he would finish it now, as there wasn't much more to do.

He attached the brakes, front and back, and tightened them up.

Curane jumped onto the bike and was off, leaving Toska to work on the windmill. He could hear the ringing of the bell as she disappeared into the distance.

Curane cycled back to the tower. At the opening there was just enough room to store her bicycle.

She was greeted by a small male with blue piercing eyes and large ears. He wore the strangest of clothes. Curane was taken aback, as she had never seen this man before. He placed his arm across the entranceway as if to stop her from entering the tower.

He wasn't going to let her past.

CHAPTER 14

"EXCUSE ME, DO I KNOW YOU? IS THERE SOMETHING I CAN help you with?"

The little man grinned at Curane. His front teeth were black, and a few of them were missing. He smelt like he hadn't washed in weeks. His hair was spiked with grey bits protruding through.

He leant forward to touch her face, and she pushed him away. His hands were small, and his nails were long and black. "Curane, I've been watching you."

Curane was scared. She turned around and began to run, fleeing towards one of the thatched huts opposite. She ran to the nearest one, which was occupied by Abby and her daughter Brom.

Abby came to the door.

"Abby, please let me in. There is a man after me, and he is really strange- looking. He said he has been watching me. He even knew my name."

Abby took Curane by the hand and guided her into their home.

The hut was very spacious inside. It was round. The fire was burning bright, which enabled them to see each other quite easily.

Brom was seated by the fire. She was younger than Curane and wore dungarees with a brightly coloured shirt. With short red hair and freckles to match, she was a pretty girl and seemed alarmed at the commotion that had just taken place. Brom rose from the chair and went over to Curane. With a sympathetic look, she took her guest's hand and sat her down by the fire. Abby was looking out of the window to see if Curane's intruder was anywhere in sight.

Curane was shaking as Brom passed her a drink.

"There's no one there now. It's all quiet." Abby came away from the window and seated herself next to Curane. "You must stay here until Toska comes back."

Toska was outside the tower. He had made his way home and had seen the small, untidy man leave the tower and head into the trees.

He wondered where Curane was as he passed the bicycle and went up the staircase to their living quarters.

It was getting dark, and the tower was glowing. Toska could be seen from the window. Abby noticed he was home.

She walked with Curane across the green towards the tower. They waved to Toska. He could see them approaching.

He came down to greet them. Curane told him what had happened. Toska was certain the man had gone into the trees. He told Curane to stay with Abby at the tower while he went into the trees to see if he could find the man. Toska was carrying a lamp and was able to see quite clearly the path into the woods. He followed the path, which took him into the thicket. He could see in the distance a small igloo-shaped hut made of straw and clay. He wondered if that was where the man had gone.

Intending to investigate, Toska walked over to the hut, and there he was the small man with the large ears and blue piercing eyes. The man had seen Toska before and held out his hand to shake his. His nails were long and dirty. Toska wasn't happy to accept the man's greeting.

"I haven't come here to make friends. I want to know why you have been following Curane."

The man frowned with disapproval. "I haven't been following her. I have been watching her. I have been watching her for a while now, and I have made my home here so I could be near her. I didn't mean to frighten her. I didn't want her to run away. I have something to tell her. She may not believe me, but I am her father."

"What on earth makes you think that?"

"I had a test done, and it came back compatible. I am 100 per cent her father. See, I have some papers."

The man passed the papers to Toska. They looked like the real thing. One of them even had the man's photo on it and Curane's. Those blue piercing eyes gave him away too. Toska had seen them so often.

Toska was concerned. He wasn't sure that Curane was going to be happy about this. After all, the man wasn't an ideal-looking father. And where had he been all these years? He looked like he had suffered a lot. The lines on his face were of deep emotion and worry.

"Does she have a mother?" Toska asked.

The man nodded his head. "She passed on a long time ago."

"Why did you not approach her in a more affectionate way instead of frightening her?"

"I don't know!" the man said, looking down and appearing to be despondent. "I didn't really know what to do."

The man was obviously distraught. Toska began to feel some warmth towards him.

The photo stated that his name was Crane Rosebury. Curane must have been given the feminine equivalent. *Crane Rosebury.* Toska repeated the name in his mind.

Curane Rosebury. Yes, he liked that. *It suits her,* he thought.

"Well, Crane, I think you had better stay here tonight. I will go home and tell Curane all about you and wait and see what the outcome will be. I will come and see you tomorrow. If Curane wishes to see you, I will bring her with me."

Crane smiled a black toothless grin.

Toska made his way home. Curane and Abby had sat patiently, awaiting his return.

He climbed the stairs to the tower and wondered how he should tell Curane about her father.

Abby left after Toska had made it clear that all was well and that she would be safe to go home.

Toska held Curane's hand as she looked into his concerned face. He began to tell her all about the man who was her father.

"So my mother isn't here then?" she queried. "No. He never mentioned what happened to her."

"That strange-looking man is my father? It's hard to believe. I always thought that my father would be tall and handsome. I wonder why I never stayed with him, or them. And why did I end up with Sly's family? I don't even remember my parents. I must have been very young when they decided to part with me."

Curane was asking all these questions which Toska couldn't answer, but he was willing to listen and to agree or disagree, whichever made sense.

Curane decided that it would be a good idea to go and see her father tomorrow, even if it was just to get some answers.

She and Toska retired to bed, but sleep didn't come to Curane easily. She was disturbed about what was going to happen the following day.

Before she knew it, the morning came. She had nodded off just before the sun came up. Feeling tired, she decided to sleep a while longer.

Toska was up and ready to face the consequences of the father–daughter meeting.

Curane was sleeping. Toska decided it was time to go and meet Crane. He touched her head very gently with his fingertips. She stirred and opened her crystal-blue eyes.

"Is it time to get up? It must be. It was time ages ago, and I went back to sleep." She yawned.

"Father, dear Father. What on earth am I doing going to see this wretched man?"

Curane was talking to herself. Toska wasn't listening. He had gone into the bathroom to finish getting washed and dressed.

Curane dressed and tidied her hair to make herself look slightly presentable. She didn't really care about her appearance today. After all, her father had already seen her a few times apparently.

"Toska, I'm ready. Let's go and get this thing over with."

Toska was still cleaning his teeth. He swished the water round in his mouth and spat it into the basin pot.

"Coming."

They both left the tower and walked through the thicket towards Crane's clay and straw home.

He was waiting outside, wearing the unclean clothes he had worn the previous day. His hair was looking spiky and dirty. Curane didn't want to hug or touch him. In fact, the sight of him repulsed her.

Why did this horrible-looking man have to be her father?

He walked towards her and smiled, his black gapped teeth showing no sign of hygienic health.

"Curane, I am so happy to be able to speak to you. I have been meaning to approach you for a long time now, but you disappeared for a while, so I wasn't able to. You lived with Slyster. I knew you then."

"Slyster. You knew Slyster?" Curane was taken aback.

"Yes, I knew Slyster. We used to fish together on the river. He didn't know who I was, but I knew he was your partner and that you had grown up together. He talked about you all the time and shared stories with me, which made me feel closer to you. In the end I decided I had to get some proof to show you that I was your father, so I took some of your fingerprints from something Slyster had of yours. Then you went away somewhere with him and came back with this young man." Crane looked at Toska with disapproval.

"Slyster was a good friend of mine."

"How could Slyster have been a good friend of yours? He never mentioned you or even talked about having met anyone when we went fishing together.

"Curane, I just want you to know that I am your father. You were looked after by people who cared for you because your mother and I were unable to."

Curane wasn't really surprised at what her father was saying, as he looked like he was unable to look after himself, never mind a young child.

"I would like to become a part of your life now, if that is possible, and try to make up for the time I have spent without you."

Curane wasn't too sure whether she wanted this man in her life. He smelt funny, he had horrible teeth and dirty hair, and his smile gave her the most uncomfortable feeling. His nails were grotesque.

She sat down on the ground, and the others followed.

Curane sat staring at this new person who had come into her life.

"I'm sorry. I think I need more time to think about all this. Can you tell me what happened to my mother?"

"Your mother was a beautiful woman, Curane, just like you."

Curane wondered why she had married such a strange-looking man if she was so beautiful.

"She passed away when you were very young, and I was left to look after you. I couldn't do it, you see. I have this disease that stunts my growth and alters my features. It is debilitating and often leaves me feeling very tired and weak.

"I haven't always looked like this."

Curane was now beginning to feel sorry for him.

He smiled at her with his black toothless grin. Curane returned the smile. "Your mother drowned while swimming in the ocean. Her body was never found, but she was lost and presumed dead. She wasn't a very good swimmer, you see. We met when we were very young, and you came along quite quickly."

Curane wanted to know more about her mother. She spent the next few hours asking questions and wanting answers, but in the end it was like most families. They were just ordinary people wanting a life of simple things and a nice family.

"You met Sly when you were very young, and you got along so well that I decided to leave you with him and his parents. You were so happy with them. I heard Slyster has passed on."

"Yes, he did. We buried him at sea. "Toska is my new partner now!"

She made it sound so cold and uncaring, like Slyster hadn't meant anything to her.

It was time to go. Curane started to walk away. She turned and told Crane that she would see him again but wasn't sure when. She just wanted to get away.

Toska wasn't far behind as they made their way to the windmill.

CHAPTER 15

THE SAILS WERE TURNING IN THE WIND, AND THE WHEEL BEGAN rattling away with the flow of the river. Curane liked to visit the windmill; it was peaceful in a strange kind of way. She could hear the sails and cogs turning, but it was a sound she had grown to love. It reminded her of progress and not death or the end of an era. She knew that while those sails were turning and when the cogs and wheels were moving, life was improving.

Toska smiled. There were no words. He had nothing to say about Crane. He knew now it was up to Curane to decide what she was going to do regarding their father–daughter relationship.

Curane smiled back. They hugged for a while, just standing still in complete silence on the bank beside the windmill, their hearts beating together as one, their breath taking in the air with the morning dew.

He brushed the hair back from her forehead and kissed it as she closed her eyes and felt the warmth of his lips.

Tears filled her eyes as she thought about Slyster, her father, and the happiness she had now found with Toska. She felt overwhelmed as a tear came down her cheek. He gently wiped it away.

"Come on, let's go home. The windmill is working fine. I think you should get some rest. You didn't sleep too well last night."

Curane looked at Toska in agreement. She slid her arm into his. They walked along the path towards the tower.

Abby was outside. They waved to her as they passed, heading towards the tower.

Mushrooms were growing in the ground. Abby began to pick them. She was carrying a basket made from the remnants of the thatching. The mushrooms were edible and mostly enjoyable. She would bake them in the pots made with clay and straw, the same materials used to build some of the huts as it was in abundance.

Curane put her head down. Toska decided he would join her.

They slept for a few hours and were awakened by the sound of a storm. It lit up the sky. They could see the flashes of lightning through the transparent tower.

Curane shook her body as the noise gave her a feeling of nervousness. Storms were frequent of late, and they weren't seeming to get any lighter.

The weather was changing as if repeated cycles of disasters were going to happen.

The flashes of lightning and cracks of thunder were becoming more frequent. The rain suddenly came down like giant drops falling from crystal rivers.

The sky lit up like a giant explosion of meteors fallen from heavenly bodies. The colours were of a rainbow. There were small lights, multicolour sparks, hovering over the tower.

Toska jumped up and looked out above the tower. He could see all the colours spiral around the tower in a circle of dance.

Curane looked up above and witnessed this enchanting sight.

The lights spun faster as they swirled into a never-ending chain. Then they stopped and shot off into the distance.

With the rain still coming down heavily, Toska drew the blinds, which he had made from old materials he had found in one of the abandoned stores. He thought he should have drawn the blinds before they'd decided to sleep, but if he had, then he would have missed that beautiful sight made by the freakish systems of a changing world.

Curane smiled. "That was magnificent. All those beautiful colours reminded me of when we used to have rainbows."

Toska was smiling too, although he had been a little apprehensive at first because he wasn't sure what was happening.

They could hear the sound of the rain outside as it beat against the tower like a lost soul.

The night was drawing in, and the rain began to pound against the tower. Toska was happy. He could visualise the river flowing at full ebb, which would help the functioning of the windmill.

Curane just lay on the bed with her eyes open, staring up at the night sky.

She thought about her father and how he would be sitting in his little mud hut alone, maybe even hungry or cold. Perhaps she would go and see him tomorrow and invite him up to the tower. Yes, she would do that. It would be the right thing to do. She was warming up to him.

Toska and Curane could hear the thunder faintly in the distance as they closed their eyes. They slept till morning.

Today was going to be a good day, or so they thought.

As they wandered over to Crane's, they could see a person on the ground lying outside his hut. It was him. They dashed over quickly and tried to lift him up, as there was no movement coming from his body. "He's gone, Curane."

Curane was rather taken aback. She had just gotten to know this man who had declared his paternity, and now he was gone, lying in a pool of water outside this little mud hut.

"We should have taken him home."

"He may have still passed away, Curane. Let's put him back in his hut. He may be at rest there."

They placed him inside the hut and covered the opening with some straw. Toska said he would make a plaque with Crane's name on it and place it over the hut.

Curane felt very sad. She was now well and truly orphaned. She'd thought it couldn't have lasted anyway. Being without parents was something she had learnt to live with.

It felt a little unusual that she had found her father and lost him in the same week. She thought about his body lying in that hut and wondered if it was the right thing to do to leave him there without burying him. But in a way he was buried in his own home where he had once lived. He would decompose and dissolve into the ground.

Humankind had come from the dust of the ground and would go back to the dust of the ground. Crane's body would be without spirit, as his spirit would have risen to higher ground.

People over the years had been buried in various places, so why couldn't her father be left where he was? It wasn't really a problem. She was just making it into one.

CHAPTER 16

TOSKA AND CURANE HEADED BACK HOME.
THINGS NEEDED TO change. People wanted to get involved in lots of projects, and Curane hadn't been helping them to evolve. She had been a little bit lax of late.

It was time to think of some new ideas again and to try to forget about the last few days. It was good to know that she knew a bit more about her parents, but living without them wasn't something new. It was something she was used to. The others had plans to work on building a raft so they would be able to transport goods downstream. Curane was going to get involved in this project. It was something she was eager to help with.

They had made plans and chopped logs and collected rope and slats, which were piled up outside the windmill. People were asking eagerly when they would be starting. It was time.

Curane gathered all the enthusiastic groups together, and they made their way to the windmill. This project was going to take her mind off things, and she was going to enjoy doing it.

Everyone was keen to get started as the raft was going to be very useful for transporting goods upriver or downriver and for travel to and fro.

The raft consisted of twelve logs, each eleven feet in length and twelve inches in diameter, and of four additional logs, each seven feet in length and ten inches in diameter.

There was one hundred feet of rope, six sheets of Styrofoam, and five wooden slats, each ten feet long. Starting with the shorter logs with flattened tops, the crew placed the longer longs placed on top in the opposite direction, followed by the shorter logs again for support. All were tied together with rope.

Flipped over, the deck was then supported with Styrofoam sheets, which were placed between the support logs, followed by the wooden slats.

A pole was then needed to steer the raft.

Most of the tops of the logs had been flattened with a knife so as to prevent them from rolling. The rope had been tied tightly and finished with an overhand knot.

The raft was soon finished.

Curane and Toska would be the first to try it out. The others slid the raft into the water. Toska held on to the pole.

They began their journey downstream.

They could feel the warmth of the sun on their faces, and they felt happy to be able to steer the raft along the way.

Toska began to sing. Curane hadn't heard him sing before, and she recognised the tune from when she was very young. He was in good spirits. She hadn't seen him this happy in a long while.

He smiled at Curane. As he looked around the raft, he felt pleased with their accomplishment.

"Well, it hasn't sunk yet, and there doesn't seem to be any water coming in.

Toska was feeling relaxed, and the water looked inviting. He pulled over to the side and tied the raft to a branch from a fallen tree while Curane laid the pole down flat.

"I'll race you to the other side!" he shouted.

They both dived into the water fully dressed. Toska was taken by a beam of light.

It happened quicker than the blinking of an eye. No sooner had he gone then Curane felt a warm glow.

She began to feel her body lift upward into this bright light. It was happening again, only this time she was more aware of the brightness of the light, and she was alone.

On arriving into the craft, she was greeted by the same distinctive aliens as before, small with oval-shaped eyes, only this time one of them smiled. He looked into her face with his dark eyes. As she glanced into them, she saw a flicker of light.

A hand opened up out to her, and she took it, responding like some child being taken away by a welcoming stranger. Without a word spoken, she knew that this creature was somehow familiar, someone she had known previously.

She felt the roughness of his skin, and the warmth of his breath on her face. He spoke in a whisper, telling her not to be afraid and that all would be well.

Curane felt safe. She knew then that this alien, this being who had welcomed her into this unknown craft, was her beloved Slyster.